The HOPPAMELEON

For Careoleeine and frog-lovers
shorter than a table

THE HOPPAMELEON
A RED FOX BOOK 0 09 940853 8

First published in Great Britain by Hutchinson,
an imprint of Random House Children's Books

Hutchinson edition published 2001
Red Fox edition published 2002

1 3 5 7 9 10 8 6 4 2

© Paul Geraghty 2001

Red Fox Books are published by Random House Children's Books,
61–63 Uxbridge Road, London W5 5SA, a division of The Random House Group Ltd,
in Australia by Random House Australia (Pty) Ltd, 20 Alfred Street, Milsons Point, Sydney, NSW 2061, Australia,
in New Zealand by Random House New Zealand Ltd, 18 Poland Road, Glenfield, Auckland 10, New Zealand,
and in South Africa by Random House (Pty) Ltd, Endulini, 5A Jubilee Road, Parktown 2193, South Africa

THE RANDOM HOUSE GROUP Limited Reg. No. 954009
www.randomhouse.co.uk

A CIP catalogue record for this book is available from the British Library.

Printed in Singapore by Tien Wah Press [PTE]

The HOPPAMELEON

PAUL GERAGHTY

RED FOX

Long before you were born, when the world was still quite young, there was a sleepy, slurpy swamp. And as the dozy insects buzzed above the water, a very odd-looking creature swam below.

Then, its beautiful eyes popped up.

The world was filled with colour. So out hopped the creature, all green and glossy, and started to chirp, 'Calling anyone like me! I'm looking for a friend! Calling anyone like me!'

When something tasty landed nearby, the chirping stopped. Its huge mouth opened, and out shot a long, sticky tongue ...

... which hit another long, sticky tongue.

'Who do you think you are,' bellowed the chameleon, 'trying to steal my dinner?'

'I-I don't know,' said the very odd-looking creature. 'I'm just looking for a friend. Who do *you* think I am?'

'Well,' the chameleon grumbled, 'you catch food with a long, sticky tongue like mine and I'm a chameleon, so you must be some kind of chameleon too. Now hop it. This is *my* patch!'

'Then I'm a chameleon,' chirped the very odd-looking creature, 'because I can hunt like a chameleon. And I'm just looking for a chameleon friend.'

'But you're hopping just like I do,' said a grasshopper, 'so you must be some kind of grasshopper too.'

'You're right,' said the very odd-looking creature. 'In that case, I must be a *hoppa*meleon.' And with a splash, it dived back into the swamp.

'Blooble-blooble, I'm a hoppameleon!' blurbled the very odd-looking creature,
'because I can
    hop like a grasshopper
    and hunt like a chameleon.
And I'm just looking for a hoppameleon friend.'

'But you can swim like I do,' bubbled a passing turtle,
'so you must be some kind of turtle too.'
'Then I must be a *turtle*hoppameleon!'
sang the very odd-looking creature,
leaping from the water ...

... and splashing a thirsty parrot.

'Hey!' yelled the parrot. 'Who do you think you are, splashing my drink all over me?'

'I'm a turtlehoppameleon,' sang the very odd-looking creature, 'because I can
swim like a turtle,
hop like a grasshopper,
and hunt like a chameleon.
And I'm just looking for a turtlehoppameleon friend.'

'But you can chirp like I do,' said the parrot, who had stopped drinking, 'so you must be some kind of parrot too.'

'Then I must be a *parrot*turtlehoppameleon!' announced the very odd-looking creature, bounding off ...

... and landing beside a stealthy lizard.

'Woah!' yelled the lizard. 'Who do you think you are, frightening away my food like that?'

'I'm a parroturtlehoppameleon,' explained the very odd-looking creature, 'because I can

chirp like a parrot,

swim like a turtle,

hop like a grasshopper,

and hunt like a chameleon.

And I'm just looking for a parroturtlehoppameleon friend.'

'But you cling with padded feet just like mine,' said
the lizard, 'so you must be some kind of lizard too.'
   'Well, then I must be a *lizzy*parroturtlehoppameleon,'
exclaimed the very odd-looking creature,

'because I can
cling like a lizard,
chirp like a parrot,
swim like a turtle,
hop like a grasshopper,
and hunt like a chameleon.
And I'm just looking for a
lizzyparroturtlehoppameleon friend.'

'But you have beautiful big eyes like mine,' interrupted a bushbaby, 'so you must be some kind of bushbaby too!'

'Then I must surely be a *baby*lizzyparroturtlehoppameleon,'
said the very odd-looking creature, almost out of breath,
'because I can
see like a bushbaby,
cling like a lizard,
chirp like a parrot,
swim like a turtle,
hop like a grasshopper,
and hunt like a chameleon.'

'And that must be the longest name in the whole of the animal kingdom.'
    The very odd-looking creature sighed.
'But I would swap all of my names
    for just *one* friend.'

Next hop, the very odd-looking creature landed
right in front of another just like itself.
'I'm a babylizzyparroturtlehoppameleon!'
said the very odd-looking creature.
'What are you?'
The other one looked for a moment,
then opened its huge mouth and said ...

'*So am I!* Let's go hopping together!'

And off they bounced, their rubbery feet making a most peculiar *Frog! Frog! Frog!* noise on the lily pads as they went.

Babylizzyparroturtlehoppameleons later got a much shorter
name, but I can't for the life of me remember what that name is,
or where it came from.
Can you?